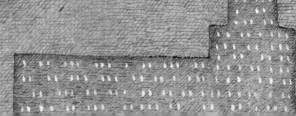

JANETTA OTTER-BARRY BOOKS

Dreams of Freedom copyright © Amnesty International UK Section 2015
Text copyright © the individual authors as named 2015
Illustrations copyright © the individual artists as named 2015
Foreword copyright © Michael Morpurgo 2015
Published by Frances Lincoln Children's Books in association with Amnesty International UK

Additionally: Clare Balding quote from *My Animals and Other Family* by Clare Balding, copyright © Clare Balding 2012.
Used by permission of The Penguin Press, a division of Penguin Group (USA) LLC.
Anne Frank quote from *The Diary of a Young Girl* by Anne Frank, edited by Otto Frank and Mirjam Pressler, translated by
Susan Massotty (Viking 1997). Copyright © The Anne Frank-Fonds, Basle, Switzerland, 1991. English translation copyright
© Doubleday a division of Bantam Doubleday Dell Publishing Group Inc, 1995.
Malala quote from *I Am Malala* by Malala Yousafzai reproduced with permission of Curtis Brown Group Ltd,
London, on behalf of Malala Yousafzai. Copyright © Malala Yousafzai 2013.
Nelson Mandela quote from *A Long Walk to Freedom* by Nelson Mandela, published by Little, Brown and Company (1994).
Jack Mapanje quote from *And Crocodiles Are Hungry at Night* by Jack Mapanje, copyright © Jack Mapanje 2011,
published by Ayebia Clarke Publishing Ltd.
Translation of Elsa Wiezell's poem copyright © Susan Smith Nash

First published in Great Britain and in the USA in 2015 by
Frances Lincoln Children's Books, 74-77 White Lion Street, London N1 9PF
www.franceslincoln.com

A catalogue record for this book is available from the British Library.

ISBN 978-1-84780-453-2

Printed in China

5 7 9 8 6 4

DREAMS of FREEDOM

IN WORDS and PICTURES

Frances Lincoln
Children's Books

in association with Amnesty International UK

Christopher Corr

Foreword

I have grown up, not in a perfect country by any means, but in a society where, by and large, we can say what we like, write what we like, be who we want to be, so long as we do not threaten the liberty of others and so long as we respect their rights. Our laws are there to defend those rights, that liberty. What we can forget, if we are not careful, is that it was not always like this. These rights have been fought for, died for, argued over, for centuries. Indeed the struggle to protect and defend our freedom goes on, both in our own country and in the world beyond.

Amnesty has been upholding these rights wherever they are threatened, challenging tyranny and injustice wherever they find it, alerting us to it. They support the downtrodden, the oppressed, those wrongly imprisoned and those who do not have human rights at all, those whose lives and liberty are in peril. It is all too easy for us to take our rights for granted, to assume the struggle is over. But Amnesty is there to remind us that it is not over, that vigilance is vital, that the fight for justice must go on. It is the good fight, and one in which all of us must be involved.

Children, perhaps better than the rest of us, understand the principle of fair play: that we should treat others with dignity and respect, as we should like to be treated ourselves. We all have a great deal to learn from children.

In its work for young people, Amnesty sets great value on the power of stories to develop empathy and broaden horizons. *Dreams of Freedom* is a feast of visual stories – brave words and beautiful pictures, woven together to inspire young readers to stand up for others and to make a difference. It gives me great hope for the freedom of future generations.

Michael Morpurgo, author and former Children's Laureate

FREEDOM TO DREAM

To achieve great things,
we must dream as well as do.

ANATOLE FRANCE

Shirin Adl

Freedom to be a child

Children are neither the property of their parents nor even the world.

BIRGITTA SIF

They belong only to their
own future freedom.

MIKHAIL BAKUNIN

I DON'T MIND IF I HAVE TO SIT ON THE FLOOR AT SCHOOL AND I AM AFRAI.

Freedom from fear

The only real prison is fear, and the only
real freedom is freedom from fear ...
You should never let your fears prevent you
from doing what you know is right.

AUNG SAN SUU KYI

Alexis Deacon

Freedom to be yourself

Freedom of expression

When I draw, it is as if a voice
is shouting inside me.

ALI FERZAT

Freedom to enjoy life and liberty

Oh, I will love the day when I break out of this cage,

Jackie Morris

Escape this solitary exile and sing wildly.

NADIA ANJUMAN

over parks carpeted with children and violets.

ARMANDO VALLADARES

mordicai Gerstein

FREEDOM FROM SLAVERY

When I found I had crossed that line,
I looked at my hands to see if I was
the same person now I was free.
There was such a glory over everything;
the sun came like gold through the trees,
and over the fields, and I felt like
I was in Heaven.

HARRIET TUBMAN

Freedom through equality

My hand is not the color of yours.
But if I pierce it, I shall feel pain.
If you pierce your hand you also feel pain.
The blood that will flow from mine will be
the same color as yours. I am a man.
The same God made us both.

CHIEF STANDING BEAR OF THE PONCA TRIBE

R. Gregory Christie

Freedom to have your own ideas

I know what I want, I have a goal,

an opinion ... Let me be myself

and then I am satisfied.

ANNE FRANK

Javier Zabala

Dale Blankenaar

FREEDOM TO FEEL SAFE

I FEEL MOST AT HOME WHEN IT'S RAINING.
NOT TOO LOUD, BUT WHEN IT'S FALLING SLOWLY.
I LIKE TO SIT AND WATCH IT. BACK AT HOME IN
AFRICA IT CAME WHEN THE LEAVES WERE GREEN.

THE WORLD IS VERY ROUGH. I LIKE IT WHEN IT'S
GENTLE AND CALM AND PEACEFUL. IT CAN'T
ALWAYS BE LIKE THAT, BUT THAT'S WHAT I LIKE.

JACK MAPANJE

FREEDOM TO HAVE A HOME

One day we will return to our homeland snug and warm in our hopes. . . . .

Raouf Karray

Oh, heart, no matter how far the winds scatter us
we will return to our homeland.

HARUN HASHIM AL-RASHID

FREEDOM THROUGH PEACE

Human beings have the right
to pursue happiness and live
in peace and freedom.

THE DALAI LAMA

Sally Morgan

FREEDOM TO TAKE RESPONSIBILITY

I have walked that long road to freedom.
I have tried not to falter; I have made missteps
along the way. But I have discovered the secret
that after climbing a great hill, one only finds
that there are many more hills to climb.
I have taken a moment here to rest, but I can
only rest for a moment, for with freedom
come responsibilities, and I dare not linger,
for my long walk is not ended.

NELSON MANDELA

Shane Evans

FREEDOM TO MAKE A DIFFERENCE

It is better to light a candle
than to curse the darkness.

CHINESE PROVERB THAT INSPIRED
AMNESTY'S VISION

PROTECT OUR HUMAN RIGHTS

CHRIS RIDDELL

Like an enormous wave

that lies down over my heart.

Like the stunning beauty of the wind over the pines.

Like an immense, vital heartbeat.

Like the moon and the river trapped by love.

Like all the dreams in the space of the eyes.

Like a fistful of infinite light.

That is the way I love freedom!

ELSA WIEZELL

Choi Jung-In

About the authors and illustrators

Christopher Corr is a British artist who studied at the Royal College of Art. His gouache illustrations are inspired by his round-the-world travels, and his vibrant picture books include *Don't Spill the Milk*, *The Goggle-Eyed Goats* and *My Granny Went to Market: a round-the-world counting rhyme.*

Anatole France (1844-1924) was the pseudonym of Jacques Anatole Thibault, a French writer with a vast literary output and a deep interest in social issues. He won the Nobel Prize for Literature in 1921.

Shirin Adl was born in Essex and raised in the newly revolutionised Iran. She is a winner of the Hallmark M&S Talented Designer Award and her books include *Pea Boy*, *Shahnameh*, *Let's Celebrate*, *Ramadan Moon* and *The Book of Dreams.*

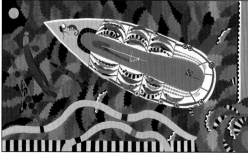

Mikhail Bakunin (1814-1876) was a Russian writer and anarchist, interested in concepts of equality and freedom, He spent many years in prison for his writing.

Birgitta Sif is an Icelandic children's book author and illustrator, educated in fine arts and illustration at Cornell University, New York and Cambridge School of Arts. Her first book, *Oliver*, was shortlisted for the Kate Greenaway Medal in 2014.

Malala Yousafzai is a Pakistani campaigner for girls' right to education. When she was 15 she was shot in the head by the Taliban. She survived and now lives in the UK, where she continues to campaign.

Roger Mello is a Brazilian illustrator, writer and playwright who has illustrated over 100 books, 20 of which he has also written. Mello is a winner of numerous prizes, most notably the 2014 Hans Christian Andersen Award for Illustration.

Aung San Suu Kyi won the Nobel Peace Prize in 1991 for her non-violent struggle for democracy and human rights in Burma, where she spent nearly two decades under house arrest.

Alexis Deacon is a British illustrator whose picture book *Beegu* was shortlisted for the Kate Greenaway Medal and selected for the New York Times Best Illustrated Children's Books award, while *Slow Loris* was shortlisted for the Blue Peter Book Award. His most recent picture book is *Cheese Belongs to You!*

Clare Balding is one of Britain's leading broadcasters and presenters. She is also an award-winning writer and retired amateur jockey.

Antje von Stemm is a German illustrator and author. Most of her books demand the reader to join in: she is an expert on unusual and creative handicraft. She has been awarded distinguished prizes: The German Youth Literature Prize for *Fräulein Pop and Mrs. Up*, the LUCHS for *Extrembasteln* and the White Raven for *On Our Boat* to name just a few. Antje shares her workspace with ten other creatives in the Hamburg studio 'Atelier Freudenhammer'.

Ali Ferzat is a Syrian political cartoonist whose work has earned him death threats and violent attack. In 2011 he was awarded the Sakharov Prize for freedom of thought and in 2012 he was named one of the 100 most influential people in the world by Time magazine.

Barroux is a French illustrator whose work has appeared in the New York Times, the Washington Post and Forbes Magazine. His most recent children's books are *My Dog Thinks I'm a Genius* and an acclaimed graphic novel for teens, *Line of Fire*.

Nadia Anjuman (1980-2005) was a poet and journalist in Afghanistan, where women have few rights. Her husband beat her to death for shaming the family by writing poetry about the oppression of Afghan women.

Jackie Morris is a British author and illustrator who lives in Wales. Her bestselling picture books include *The Ice Bear*, *The Snow Leopard* and *Song of the Golden Hare*, as well as a ypoung adult novel, *East of the Sun, West of the Moon* which was nominated for the Branford Boase Award.

Armando Valladares is a Cuban artist who spent 22 years in prison and became an Amnesty prisoner of conscience. After torture, he was confined to a wheelchair for several years.

Ros Asquith is a British illustrator and writer who has been a Guardian cartoonist for twenty years. She was shortlisted for the Roald Dahl Funny Prize with *Letters from an Alien Schoolboy* and is the illustrator of *The Great Big Book of Families*, written by Mary Hoffman, which won the SLA Information Book Award.

Harriet Tubman (c.1832-1913) was an African American woman who was born into slavery. She escaped and underwent many dangers to help free other slaves through the Underground Railroad.

Mordicai Gerstein is an American writer and illustrator of over thirty children's books, and winner of the 2004 Caldecott Medal for his post 9/11 picture book *The Man Who Walked Between the Towers*.

Chief Standing Bear (1829-1908) was a Native American Ponca chief. He brought a lawsuit against the US Army for ejecting his people from their homelands. In a landmark judgement, Indians were recognised as 'persons' entitled to legal rights and protection.

R. Gregory Christie is an American illustrator and three-times winner of the Coretta Scott King Honor Award in Illustration. His most recent picture book, *It Jes' Happened*, was an Ezra Jack Keats Award Honor Book. He has illustrated more than 50 books, a multitude of magazine images and many Jazz album covers.

Anne Frank (1929-1945) was one of over a million Jewish children who died in the Nazi Holocaust. When in hiding she wrote a diary that was discovered after her death. It has become one of the most famous diaries of all time.

Javier Zabala is a Spanish writer and illustrator whose book *El Soldadito Salomon* won the National Illustration Prize for the best illustrations in children's literature. In 2014 Zabala was selected for the Ilustrarte Biennial International Award.

Jack Mapanje is a Malawian-born poet, writer and academic. Jailed without charge for nearly four years, he was declared a prisoner of conscience by Amnesty International. He now lives in the UK.

Dale Blankenaar is a South African picture book illustrator living in Cape Town. He illustrated the four-book *Animal Tales* series, published in both English and Afrikaans.

Harun Hashim al-Rashid is an award-winning Palestinian poet, born in Gaza and regarded as one of the most influential and prolific poets writing in Arabic. He has also worked as a teacher and broadcaster and as Palestinian representative to the Arab league.

Raouf Karray is a Palestinian illustrator and graphic artist who is professor of visual communication and graphic arts at the University of Sfax in Tunisia. His books are published in France, Italy and Tunisia and he is a recipient of the Noma Concours for Picture Book Illustrations Award.

The 14th Dalai Lama, Tenzin Gyatso, is a Buddhist monk and spiritual leader of Tibet. In 1989 he was awarded the Nobel Peace Prize for his non-violent struggle for Tibet's liberation from China.

Sally Morgan is an Australian Aboriginal author and illustrator of over 30 books, who is the Design Director at Karrunga Media. She won the Human Rights and Equal Opportunity Commission Humanitarian Award for *My Place*.

Nelson Mandela (1918-2013) was the first black President of South Africa, elected after spending 27 years in prison for opposing apartheid. He worked to achieve human rights for everyone in South Africa.

Shane Evans is an award-winning American illustrator of more than thirty picture books for children. His titles include *The Way a Door Closes* and *Olu's Dream*. Evans is a winner of the Coretta Scott King/John Steptoe Award and he runs a community art space in Kansas City.

This Chinese proverb inspired Peter Benenson when he founded **Amnesty International** in 1961.

Chris Riddell is a British illustrator and writer, and a political cartoonist for the Observer. A winner of two Kate Greenaway Medals, his books include the internationally bestselling series, *The Edge Chronicles*, with Paul Stewart. His illustrated novel, *Goth Girl*, won the 2013 Costa Award.

Elsa Wiezell (1926-2014) was an award-winning Paraguayan poet, artist and university teacher. In her long and prolific career she founded Asunción's Modern Art Museum, was chief editor of the journal *The Feminist* and director and founder of the Belle Arts School.

Choi Jung-In is an internationally admired Korean illustrator. Her first book, *Picture thief, Junmo*, was published in 2003 and she has now illustrated over one hundred children's books, including *Princess Bari*, *Volubilis* and *La Petite-Fille Qui Voulait Tout*.

The Universal Declaration of Human Rights tells us 'we are all born free and equal'. Human rights are fundamental rights that uphold freedom, truth, justice and fairness. They belong to all of us. This beautiful book looks at some of our freedoms.

Amnesty International is a movement of people all over the world working together to protect our human rights. We believe that standing up for freedom is right and fair and makes the world a better place. So we are very grateful to the artists and authors of this book for their inspiration and generosity.

Anyone can stand up for freedom, in many different ways. How about starting an Amnesty group at school? Find out how to get going at www.amnesty.org.uk/education

Teachers can find free downloadable human rights education activities for this book and others at www.amnesty.org.uk/fiction

Amnesty International UK
17-25 New Inn Yard
London EC2A 3EA
Tel 020 7033 1500
student@amnesty.org.uk
www.amnesty.org.uk

Amnesty International USA
5 Penn Plaza
New York NY 10001
Tel (212) 807 8400
www.amnestyusa.org

Amnesty International Canada (English speaking)
312 Laurier Avenue East
Ottawa
Ontario K1N 1H9
Tel: 1 800 266 3789
www.amnesty.ca

Amnesty International Australia
Locked Bag 23
Broadway
New South Wales 2007
Tel: 1300 300 920
www.amnesty.org.au